D0312094

This edition published by Parragon Books Ltd in 2014

Parragon Books Ltd
Chartist House
15–17 Trim Street
Bath BA1 1HA, UK
www.parragon.com

ISBN 978-1-4723-5889-9

Printed in China

Bath • New York • Cologne • Melbourne • Delhi
Hong Kong • Shenzhen • Singapore • Amsterdam

Dusty Crophopper was a racing sensation! Three years had passed since he had won the Wings Around The Globe Rally and he had been living his dream of racing.

While he loved to race, he couldn't do it alone. He often told reporters: "I've had an amazing team supporting me every step of the way."

When he wasn't racing, Dusty spent his time at home in Propwash Junction, where the annual Corn Festival would soon be held. Dusty and his friends were all excited because the Corn Festival had made national news!

Later that day, Skipper, Dusty's coach, was putting the champ through his paces. Dusty roared through turns and pulled into a steep climb.

Suddenly, Dusty's engine stuttered and he fell into a spin! "Dusty? Dusty? What's wrong?" Skipper asked worriedly.

Feeling very sick, Dusty couldn't answer. Luckily, he regained control and landed safely.

Dottie, Dusty's mechanic, had bad news. "Your gearbox is failing," she told him. Even worse, it couldn't be replaced – it was out of production. "You push yourself into the red, you crash," Dottie explained as she fitted Dusty with a warning gauge. "It comes on, you need to pull power, slow down," she said. "I'm so sorry."

That evening, Dusty was upset. He wanted to prove that he could still be a racer, so he took off into the night sky and sped across the treetops.

Suddenly, the warning light flashed and Dusty slowed down.

Dusty had been so busy staring at the warning light, he didn't realize that he was flying too close to a tall tower. He clipped the top of it, landed hard and skidded right into the airport's petrol station!

The petrol station's roof collapsed and one of the pumps exploded. KABOOM!

PROPWASH JUNCTION
HOME OF
DUSTY
WORLD RACING
CHAMPION

Mayday, the airport's fire engine, took aim at the blaze, but his leaky old fire hose didn't do much good. Desperate, he called for volunteers to help pull over the water tower.

"Pull!" yelled Mayday. "Pull!" As Mayday, Skipper, Chug and Dusty tugged, the tower creaked and groaned then fell, sending a wave of water across the tarmac. The fire was out.

The next day, two safety officials declared Propwash Junction's airport unsafe – no one was allowed to fly in or out. The airport could only be reopened once Mayday's equipment was updated and a second firefighter was found. That meant the Corn Festival would have to be cancelled! Feeling guilty, Dusty headed towards the fire station to see Mayday.

One of Mayday's old photos caught Dusty's eye. "Is this you and an old crop duster?" Dusty asked.

Mayday explained it was a SEAT – a Single Engine Air Tanker. Instead of crop dusting, a SEAT dropped water.

Suddenly Dusty knew what he had to do. He would become Propwash's new firefighter!

Bright and early the next day, Dusty flew off towards the air-attack base in Piston Peak National Park. Mayday's friend Blade Ranger, a veteran fire and rescue helicopter, had agreed to train Dusty.

Blade was the head of the base, so he knew his stuff!

Dusty landed and rolled to a stop. “Hey guys,” he called out. “What’s up? I’m Dusty.”

But no one seemed to notice. They were all doing other things....

A plane called Lil’ Dipper was busy sunning herself. She was a super-scooper, who could skim lakes and scoop up tons of water to drop onto fires and put them out.

Windlifter, a mighty heavy-lift helicopter, was busy lifting dozens of huge logs.

Cabbie, a transport plane, was carefully listening to the radio in case an emergency came in ...

... and a group of little trucks called smokejumpers were playing games!

Just then, an emergency horn blared and the air attack base sprang into action! Dusty followed them and saw that Blade Ranger was already on the scene, dumping fire retardant onto the blaze.

Blade told Windlifter to drop next. Together, they snuffed out a large part of the wildfire. Cabbie flew over the area and the smokejumpers parachuted to the ground to make sure the fire was out.

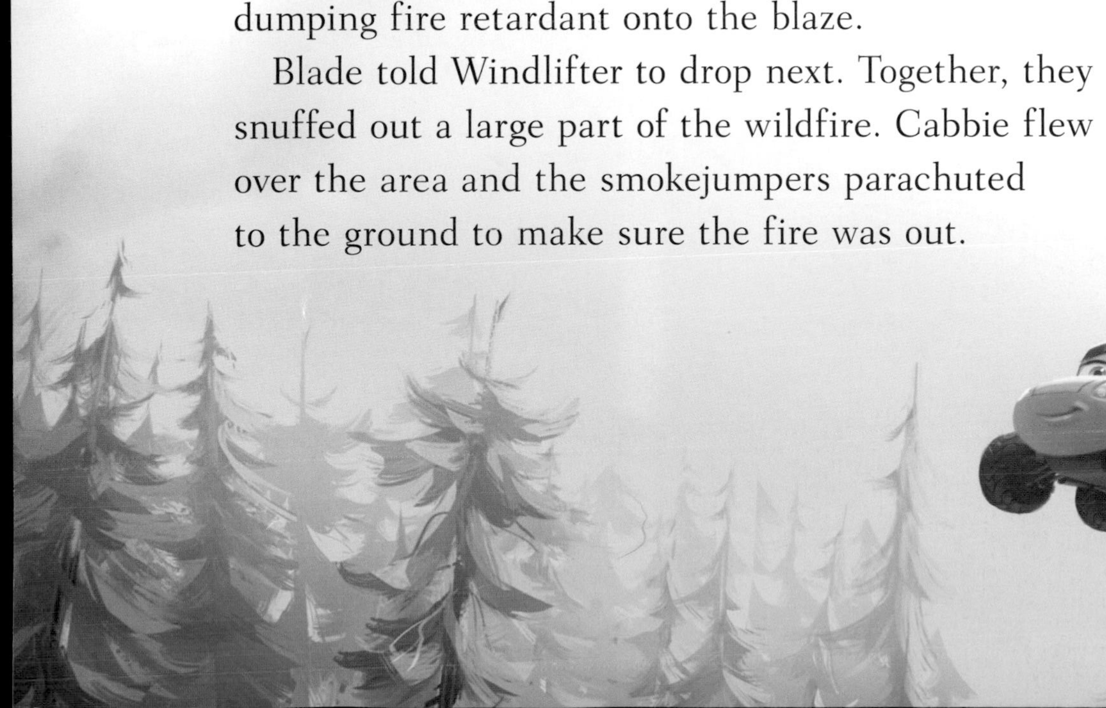

Back at base, Dusty explained that he was there to be trained.

"You're the SEAT Mayday radioed me about?" asked Blade.

"Not just some SEAT," Dipper said. "It's Dusty Crophopper!"

But Blade wasn't impressed. He told a mechanic called Maru to rip off Dusty's landing gear and replace it with pontoons. These would allow Dusty to scoop up water.

Dusty's training began. Blade taught him about different types of fire and how to fight them.

PISTON PEAK
301

Next, Blade took Dusty to Anchor Lake and gave him lessons on how to fill his pontoons. But it wasn't easy. Dusty skidded across the surface of the lake and nearly slammed into the trees!

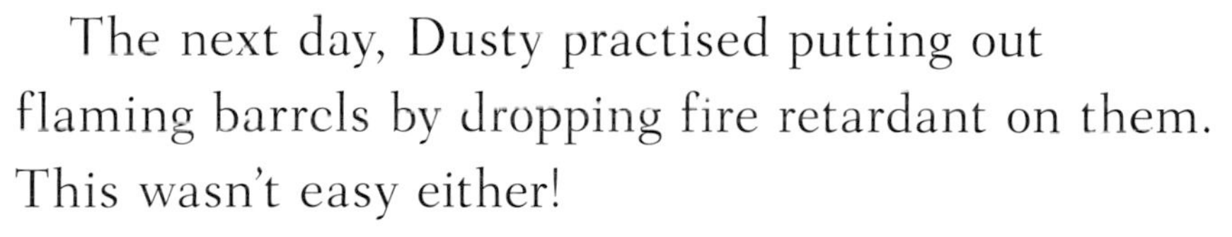

The next day, Dusty practised putting out flaming barrels by dropping fire retardant on them. This wasn't easy either!

First Dusty dropped the retardant too late. Then, he came in too low! After many tries, putting out just one of the barrels was the best that he could do.

Later, Dusty saw smoke rising from the forest. Without a second thought, he rushed in and made a perfect drop.

Blade grimaced. Dusty had put out a family campfire!

"Good job," Blade said. "You just saved those folks from a nice holiday!"

That evening, Dusty talked to his friends by radio. They had some good news – they'd found a new gearbox for him!

"We'll have it in a couple days," said Chug.

"Wow, thanks! That's the best news," Dusty replied. He couldn't have been happier.

Back outside, Dusty met Cad Spinner, the Park Superintendent. When Cad realized that Dusty was the famous racer, he excitedly invited him to the re-opening of his hotel, Fusel Lodge. The party was taking place the following evening.

Then Cad turned to Blade. "He's even more famous than you, Blazin' Blade!"

"Blazin' Blade?" Dusty repeated.

But Blade simply sighed and rolled off towards his hangar.

Later on, Dusty found out from the others that Blazin' Blade was the star of an old TV show called CHoPS – California Helicopter Patrol!

"If Blade was such a big TV star," asked Dusty, "what's he doing here?"

"Whatever the reason is, it's his business. And we're not asking," said Dynamite, one of the smokejumpers.

Overnight, a lightning storm started several fires.

"This is a big one," Blade said. "Load up!"

Dusty started to get ready, but Blade told him to stay behind.

"We need every plane," argued Windlifter.

Blade realized that Windlifter was right. They needed Dusty.

Blade directed the attack on the fires and soon had the situation under control. The smokejumpers were dropped into a clearing to help keep the fire from spreading, but then the wind changed and they became trapped!

Dipper was about to release her flame retardant to help the smokejumpers, when suddenly Dusty zoomed past her and made a drop – right on target! The smokejumpers were safe.

Later, Blade had some tough words for Dusty. "You broke formation," he said. "Don't go planning your certification party yet, champ."

As night fell, Dusty, Dipper, Windlifter and Maru – still covered in pink fire retardant – arrived at Fusel Lodge for the grand re-opening party. "Whoa," said Dusty. "Look at this place!"

"Dusty!" cried Cad. The superintendent wanted to be seen with Dusty to impress the Secretary of the Interior. "I'm up for a promotion," Cad explained.

Harvey and Winnie, two elderly RVs who were guests at the lodge, called Dusty and Dipper over. They needed a little help.

"We honeymooned here fifty years ago," Winnie told them. "And Harvey is trying to find the spot where we had our first kiss."

"That's so sweet," said Dipper. Then she smiled at Dusty.

The gang chatted a while longer. Dusty and Dipper worked out that the place they were looking for was Augerin Canyon, by Upper Whitewall Falls.

Later in the evening, Dusty and his new friends talked about firefighting.

"Maybe this fire-fighting thing will be a second career for you," Harvey said.

"You know," said Dipper, "this is a second career for all of us. Windlifter was a lumberjack and I hauled cargo."

Hearing this gave Dusty hope – maybe racing wasn't everything.

PISTON PEAK
N0626G
301
7

The next morning, Dusty was awoken by his friends from home over the radio. The gearbox they had found was the wrong one! It seemed as though Dusty's racing days were truly over.

Moments later, Maru burst into Dusty's hangar. There were two new wildfires burning and they were moving towards Fusel Lodge! Dusty and the firefighters were soon airborne. Maru radioed the lodge, telling Cad to evacuate. But Cad refused – he wouldn't let a little fire ruin his business.

As they approached the fire, Blade ordered Dusty to drop only half of his fire retardant. But Dusty wasn't paying attention. He was watching his warning light, thinking of how he would never race again.

After Blade dropped his fire retardant, Dusty dumped his, too – all of it.

Blade was furious. "Return to base!" he yelled.

But Dusty didn't return to base. Instead, he flew down to the surface of Anchor Lake and tried to reload his pontoons. But the lake was too choppy and Dusty's nose hit the water.

"My engine stalled!" he yelled. Dusty drifted downstream and into the rapids!

Blade threw down a line, but it fell short. “You need to start your engine. You can take off before the falls!” he cried.

Dusty managed to start his engine and gave it full throttle. But just as he started to lift off, his warning light flashed, so Dusty slowed down.

"Why are you holding back?" Blade yelled, unaware that Dusty's gearbox was broken.

Just then, Dusty went over the falls!

Blade swooped in and snagged Dusty in mid-air. It took all of the rescue helicopter's strength to swing Dusty to safety on the ground.

But there was no time to rest. The fire was closing in – fast!

"Follow me," said Blade.

Outside the entrance to an old mine, Blade turned angrily to Dusty. "You need to follow orders!"

"I never wanted to be a firefighter anyway," said Dusty.

"Then go back to racing!" Blade answered.

"I can't!" the crop duster admitted. "My gearbox is busted. That's why I pulled power! I'm never going to race again."

Blade sighed. "Life doesn't always go the way you expect it. But you came here to become a firefighter. If you give up today, think of all the lives you won't save tomorrow."

Blade and Dusty entered the mine just before the firestorm reached them. Flaming embers and hot smoke swirled around the entrance and Blade shielded Dusty from the heat.

After the fire had passed, Blade and Dusty rolled into a meadow. They tried to take off, but Blade was badly damaged and he crashed.

Dusty immediately radioed the base. "Blade is down! I repeat, Blade is down!"

Meanwhile, one of the fires was getting even closer to Fusel Lodge. Finally, somebody there realized that they were in real danger! The guests panicked and rushed for the exits.

Windlifter responded to Dusty's call and carried Blade home. Dusty flew alongside, hoping that his friend would be okay.

Back at the air-attack base, Cabbie, Maru and the smokejumpers were waiting. Maru quickly got to work to try to fix Blade.

Later, while the rescue helicopter rested, Maru told Dusty the reason why Blade had left his television show and come to Piston Peak....

Blade's partner on the TV show crashed while doing a stunt. Blade was there, but he didn't know how to help him. His friend never recovered, so Blade left.

"Blade ... he used to pretend to save lives," said Maru. "Now, he saves 'em for real."

At that moment, the fire was closing in on the lodge. Cad ordered André, the concierge, to send more water to the rooftop sprinklers. The firefighters needed that water, but Cad cared more about his lodge.

Meanwhile, the Secretary of the Interior worked with Pulaski, the lodge's fire engine, and a park employee called Ol' Jammer to get all the vehicles to safety.

Unfortunately, there was only one road out of Piston Peak and it led through a tunnel! Worried cars were queuing along the exit road, with the fire burning dangerously nearby.

Suddenly, there was a huge gust of wind and a wall of flame roared over the ridge! A train, who was about to leave Piston Peak through the tunnel, slammed on his brakes – the fire had blocked the entrance!

"We're gonna have to find another way out," the secretary shouted.

"That's the problem," Ol' Jammer replied. "There is no other way out."

Back at the base, Windlifter had taken command. The team flew through the fire to get to the road, then took aim at the flames. Windlifter dived down and dropped his fire retardant – a perfect strike! Dipper followed with another precision drop.

Finally Dusty released his retardant, smothering the remaining flames. The fire was out! The guests cheered as the smokejumpers moved in to open the road.

But not all the guests had escaped. Harvey and Winnie were trapped in Augerin Canyon! Dusty hurried to help them.

Suddenly Harvey began to slip! Just then Blade arrived, back in action, and threw a line to hold Harvey in place.

Dusty flew as fast as he could. His warning light flashed red, but he kept going. Then, he pulled straight up and skimmed the face of Whitewall Falls, filling his pontoons with water!

With his warning light still flashing, Dusty doused the flames. The RVs rushed to safety as the bridge collapsed behind them.

"Good move, partner," said Blade. Dusty smiled.

But then – KA-CHUNK – Dusty's gearbox gave out. He had pushed it too hard! He started to drop towards the forest.

Dusty struggled to keep himself in the air, but his propeller stopped turning and he crashed into the trees.

A few days later, Dusty, still groggy, rolled out of Maru's hanger. His firefighting friends were there to greet him.

Maru had good news for Dusty. Not only had he patched Dusty up on the outside, he used spare parts to build him a custom-made gearbox!

"I'd say you earned that certification," said Blade.

Dusty cranked the engine and his propeller sprang to life!

301
22
28
36
10

After his daring adventure, Dusty was glad to get home. While he was away, Dottie had completely updated Mayday. Now that Propwash had its two certified firefighters, it was open for business again!

The Corn Festival quickly got into full swing. Chug got on the loudspeaker. "Ladies and gentleplanes, the Propwash Junction Corn Fest is proud to present the Piston Peak Air-Attack Team, and our very own Dusty Crophopper!"

Everyone cheered their favourite firefighting, racing plane!